# The Springfield Witch

# The Springfield Witch

Mandie O'Brien

*AuthorHouse*™
*1663 Liberty Drive*
*Bloomington, IN 47403*
*www.authorhouse.com*
*Phone: 1-800-839-8640*

© 2012 by Mandie O'Brien. All rights reserved.

No part of this book may be reproduced, stored in a retrieval system, or transmitted by any means without the written permission of the author.

Published by AuthorHouse    12/10/2012

ISBN: 978-1-4772-5036-5 (sc)
ISBN: 978-1-4772-5037-2 (hc)
ISBN: 978-1-4772-5038-9 (e)

Any people depicted in stock imagery provided by Thinkstock are models, and such images are being used for illustrative purposes only.
Certain stock imagery © Thinkstock.

This book is printed on acid-free paper.

Because of the dynamic nature of the Internet, any web addresses or links contained in this book may have changed since publication and may no longer be valid. The views expressed in this work are solely those of the author and do not necessarily reflect the views of the publisher, and the publisher hereby disclaims any responsibility for them.

To the memory of Granny Shaw

Forever in our hearts

# Contents

| | | |
|---|---|---|
| Chapter One | A Beginning | 1 |
| Chapter Two | Agnes | 8 |
| Chapter Three | Ned | 17 |
| Chapter Four | Friends | 33 |
| Chapter Five | A New Witch | 49 |
| Chapter Six | An Unwelcome Visit | 61 |
| Chapter Seven | Ned Has a Solution | 69 |
| Chapter Eight | Where's Jennie? | 75 |
| Chapter Nine | More Disappearances | 83 |
| Chapter Ten | Agnes Starts Investigating | 89 |
| Chapter Eleven | Agnes in Trouble | 94 |
| Chapter Twelve | Ned in Danger | 101 |
| Chapter Thirteen | Agnes Takes Action | 106 |
| Chapter Fourteen | Mr. O'Gill Takes Action | 113 |
| Chapter Fifteen | The Villagers Get a Shock | 119 |
| Chapter Sixteen | Villagers Reunited | 126 |
| Chapter Seventeen | Agnes Returns | 138 |

# Chapter One
## A Beginning

Many, many years ago in the Irish countryside, while the autumn winds were swirling leaves and rain around the house, a mother was telling her child a bedtime story. The child, Agnes, was tucked up in a very small bed, in a very plain room. The walls of the room were bare, but as her mother, Wilhemina, related her story, the images of the tale were magically played out on the walls of the room.

It was obvious that Wilhemina was enjoying herself immensely; Agnes, on the other hand, looked bored. She stared at the ceiling, paying no attention to the images on the walls. Occasionally she picked at or chewed her nails and even made a few exaggerated yawns. Oblivious to her daughter's lack of interest, the mother went on with the story.

'Then, deep in the bowels of the Fairy Underworld, the hooded, cloaked figure silently ran along a narrow, dimly lit tunnel. Every now and again it would stop under a torch and examine an object which it held tightly in its hand. It was impossible to see what the object was, but an occasional glint of gold could be seen through the creature's dark, gnarled fingers. The tunnel seemed more like a maze, for several dark passages led off the meandering main passage. Despite the lack of light, the cloaked figure moved with surprising speed, intermittently turning into random passages, suggesting it had passed that way many times before.

'Only when it reached a tiny opening at the end of the tunnel did the figure stop. It stood for several minutes peering back into the darkness of the tunnel, as if making sure no one was following it. The strange being, obviously satisfied that it was alone, squeezed itself through the opening and stepped out into a moonlit night. Once outside, it wrapped the cloak more tightly around its oddly shaped body and sped off into the night.

'The next morning, the fairies awoke to find one of their most powerful magic artefacts missing . . . Worse than missing. It had been stolen. Stolen by a traitor. Stolen by an evil, wicked goblin called Grobbler.'

Wilhemina fell quiet, and the images on the walls faded. She sat in silence for a few moments until a very loud yawn from Agnes jerked her out of her reverie.

'Can I to go to sleep now?' Agnes asked, not even bothering to hide the boredom in her voice.

Her mother tutted loudly, pulled Agnes's blankets up to her chin, and tucked them in so tightly that the child could barely move. She lifted the candle from Agnes's bedside. As she walked to the door, she heard her daughter squirming in her bed.

'Mum, can you tell me a new story tomorrow?' asked Agnes.

'I haven't finished telling you about Grobbler, but I suppose I could tell you about Brian, King of the Leprechauns.'

'No, Mum. I mean a proper story . . . about history.'

'It is a story about history,' stated her mum firmly.

'I mean about real people.'

'Agnes, we have gone over this before. You need to know these things.'

'I won't listen to stories about fairies or leprechauns,' Agnes said defiantly as she unsuccessfully tried to hide herself under her blanket.

'Tomorrow you will hear about the leprechauns, and that's final,' said Wilhemina.

'I will not,' mumbled Agnes.

Wilhemina sighed, shook her head, and left the room, slamming the door behind her.

'I hate being a witch,' said Agnes, when she was sure she was alone.

Sitting at the fire that night, Wilhemina wondered what was ailing her daughter. She wasn't interested in tales of magic, which would be strange enough for any normal child, but for Agnes it was downright weird. Agnes wasn't a normal child; she was special. She was the latest in a long line of witches. But for some reason, Agnes didn't want to be a witch. She fought her mother at every turn and was constantly neglecting her magical studies for her school work. If she hadn't been present at her birth, Wilhemina would have doubted Agnes was her daughter.

Wilhemina hesitated for a moment before lifting her crystal ball. She was used to looking into the futures of others; after all, she was a witch, and nosiness was a perk of the job. To be honest, there wasn't a single person in her village whose future was unknown to Wilhemina. She had passed many informative and amusing hours peering into her crystal ball. But she had never looked into what the future held for Agnes; there was simply no need. Wilhemina had already planned Agnes's future to the very last detail, and despite her daughter's stubbornness she had always been sure that nothing was going to change even one aspect of her carefully laid out plans.

'Let's see what will happen if you have your way.' After peering into the ball for several minutes, she tutted and shook her head. 'No, young lady. I'm not standing for any of that.'

A glazed look came over Wilhemina's face as she stared deeper into the ball; the room was deadly still when suddenly she slammed her hand on the table so hard the crystal ball wobbled on the tripod. Wilhemina reached out and steadied it. Now she was determined. No matter what the consequences, Agnes was going to complete her training. Even if it was the last thing she did.

# Chapter Two

# Agnes

The villagers of Springfield, County Fermanagh, knew that Agnes was a witch. Being a witch wasn't something to be ashamed of. Witches in Ireland were held in high esteem. People would come from all over the surrounding countryside to consult witches on cures, curses, and, of course, fortune telling. If you had a witch living in or near your village, you would have been so proud you would brag about it to anyone you met. Those you bragged to would have looked at you in awe. Having a witch would sometimes, depending on the reputation of the witch, have gotten you a better price for your livestock at the market.

But no one bragged about Agnes. It wasn't that she was an evil witch or that she was incompetent. Although she didn't hold with casting curses, she used her magical skill to develop potions and medicines. In fact, she was a marvel. Her broccoli and barley laxative was so effective that you didn't even need to drink it; one whiff was enough to send you running for the lavatory. Judging by her potions, any intelligent person would realise that if she did decide to cast a curse, it would be very powerful and would work extremely efficiently on its sorry victim.

Springtown was a simple, traditional village, and the residents were set in their ways. They knew how things should be, and the kind of witch Agnes was went against all their traditions and beliefs. The village folk of Springfield only recognised two types of witches. The first and best were the scary ones, who lived in rundown houses full of cobwebs and dust, a cauldron containing some thick, bubbling green liquid, and shelves lined with jars of disembowelled frogs or other nasty ingredients. Then there was the other type, the beautiful witch with the pretty, fussy, flowery house. Even that at a push would have been better than Agnes, who didn't fit either of the stereotypes.

The problem with Agnes was that she was weird—but not in a good, witchy way. If you saw her walking down the street, you would take her for a schoolteacher rather than a witch. (In fact, there was a rumour that she had once been a teacher, for whenever she passed a child she was always shooting strange questions at the poor thing. Such as 'What is 150 multiplied by 43?' or 'How do you spell chrysanthemum?')

One thing the villagers knew was that witches always wore black. But Agnes never wore black. Her clothes were plain and sensible and were always navy, grey, or dark shades of brown, but never black. Also, there wasn't a wart to be seen on her, and although she wasn't pretty, she certainly wasn't ugly. She was the personification of ordinary. Her hair was neither wild and tatty nor lank and greasy; it was always pulled back into a very neat bun. Agnes wasn't grumpy or snide, and she certainly didn't cackle. Nor did she go about being extremely happy and singing pretty songs about birds and flowers.

She even attended church! What was she thinking of? Witches didn't go to church. Even Old Mother Beatrice over in Irvinestown didn't attend church, and it was well known that she did some mighty strange things. But this was much more serious than wearing your knickers on your head or building a new cottage out of cake.

To the people of Springfield, the situation was impossible. She neither acted like a witch nor looked like a witch, and she certainly didn't live like a witch. Her cottage was also a problem for them. It was a rather plain, ordinary cottage. There was nothing about it that said, 'This is a witch's cottage.' It was a very embarrassing spectacle for the residents of Springfield. But the villagers weren't going to be beaten.

Not long after she had arrived, the folks of the village sent a small group of selected representatives to address the problem. They had a friendly chat with Agnes and pointed out the little changes they thought she should make to her appearance and her cottage. But they didn't have any luck. Agnes proved to be stubborn and remained as unlike a witch as she always had.

Not to be deterred, some of the villagers snuck into her cottage when she was out and left gifts of animal skulls, scraggly looking cats, and even spiders. No one was quite sure what she did with the spiders or skulls, but the cats always found their way back to their original owners. Agnes and her cottage remained the same.

Then the men of Springfield volunteered their services as gardeners. If Agnes didn't want to be the scary witch, then they would accept the alternative. They brought roses, daisies, and apple trees, but Agnes refused to let them even dig a hole. Instead, she filled her garden with vegetables and herbs, and in place of cute kittens and rabbits she bought a nanny goat for milk.

In the end, the villagers, knowing they were beaten, gave up. They didn't accept her into their village, nor did they totally ignore her. They just treated her as they would have anyone with whom they had nothing in common: with a strained politeness. The ladies always said hello to her, and if required the men always opened doors for her. Even the children were respectful. They never played ball in front of her cottage, nor did they rap her door and run away. Of course, this was probably due more to the fact they didn't want to be quizzed on math and spelling than out of politeness or respect. But in the end the villagers were content with their compromise.

Agnes was not. She was lonely, and the bottles of her potions had started taking up all the space in her kitchen. She was distressed that the people of Springfield didn't even come to her for cures; instead, they travelled to Derrygonnelly to consult the witch there. Agnes was annoyed because she knew that Minnie's potions weren't half as good as hers. She had thought about trying to become the kind of witch they wanted, but she was sensible enough to know that she could never pull it off. It simply wasn't in her. Even though she had known what she was from practically the day she was born, it had taken her a long time to come to terms with being a witch.

When she was younger, she had even run away from home and spent six happy months as a country schoolteacher. But unfortunately, a child in her school had become seriously ill, and Agnes had used her powers to heal the girl. Of course, before you could say Jack Robinson, she was asked to hand her notice in at the school and become the village witch. She felt then she had no alternative but to return home to her mother and finish her studies in witchcraft. When she did arrive home, her mother wasn't at all surprised to see her, which made Agnes extremely suspicious that her mother had been behind the child's illness. Of course, Agnes would never ask her mother about it, mainly because she knew Wilhemina would never admit to the truth.

It was then that she realised she couldn't fight her destiny—or her mother. But she was determined not to change the person she was deep inside. Although she had accepted her fate, she had decided she would never use magic. Instead, she would be a master of medicines and potions, and she would dress and behave as she pleased. She thought that would make her happy, but after a few months living in Springfield, she was more miserable than she had ever been. It came as a shock to her when she realised she was unhappy because she was lonely. She did try to make friends, but nothing she did worked. Agnes knew she couldn't go back to her mother, so she settled into the village as best she could. No one in the village suspected she was unhappy, and they certainly never suspected that Agnes had a secret dream. It was the only thing which kept her going.

She dreamt that she had become famous for her potions and medicines. She even dreamt that she also taught in the village school and that all her pupils loved her. She didn't think her dream was unreasonable. All she needed was for the people to move with the times, but even though the world had just come into the twentieth century, Ireland still held on to its traditions. She liked that about her country, but she wished they could see her as the exception. Until that day, she would just keep dreaming and hoping that something might happen to make her dreams come true.

# Chapter Three
# Ned

Ned Kenny gathered his books from his desk and filed out of the classroom behind the other children. His first day of school hadn't been too bad. He did like his teacher, but he thought her lessons were just too easy. For instance, the words in the spelling test weren't challenging at all; Ned had been able to spell words like 'notorious' and 'immediately' for years now. He also was well past learning his seven-times tables. Ned had spent the math lesson making up his own sums. The boy called Joe who sat across from him had glanced over once and caught sight of what he was doing. Ned, fearing Joe would tell on him, cleaned his slate and spent the rest of the lesson bored.

But Ned had nothing to be worried about. Joe never said a thing about it and at lunch Joe was the only one who made an attempt to speak to him. The other children were shy around him, especially as he seemed so much smarter than even the eldest students. Ned had answered every one of the teacher's questions. Occasionally, he had his hand up even before Miss Meek had finished asking the question. The children were so intimidated by him that they didn't even make fun of him. This was unusual, especially since he wore spectacles. Jimmy Hood wore glasses, and not a day went by without someone calling him 'specky four eyes.'

Because Joe Mullen had been the only one forward enough to speak with Ned, on the walk home from school Joe found himself surrounded by children all trying to pry little bits of information from him concerning the new boy. Joe was in his element; he had never before been this popular.

'He didn't say too much,' explained Joe. But when the faces of his listeners dropped, he quickly added. 'What I mean is, he didn't say too much about school. But he did say his whole family came here to live with Mr. O'Gill. He's his dad's uncle, don't you know. His mum and dad are to help run Whitethorn Farm.'

'Where did he come from?' asked a pretty little girl called Jennie. She was especially interested in Ned, as she was always on the lookout for a new beau and Ned was a handsome young boy.

'He said he came from somewhere outside Cookstown. From a village, I think,' answered Joe, blushing. Jennie was really very pretty.

'Ooh, Cookstown,' all the children said as if speaking of a magic kingdom.

As Cookstown was in another county, it did seem magical to them. Most of them hadn't even been to Enniskillen, which was the nearest major town. They carried on walking with Joe and plying him with questions, most of which he couldn't answer and some of which he shouldn't have; for he made up more answers than he knew. The children were running out of questions, but Joe didn't want to lose his moment in the limelight.

'He had a really odd lunch with him today,' said Joe, attempting to sound mysterious. The children looked at him, wondering what he was talking about. How could a lunch be odd? They all usually had the same: an apple, a scone or a piece of wheaten bread with jam, and a bottle of milk corked with paper. Sometimes they had a hard-boiled egg, but that was usually in the winter.

'He had raw vegetables,' he added as mysteriously before.

'What do you mean, raw vegetables?' asked Jennie sharply. No way was she having a beau who ate vegetables, no matter how cute his curls and freckles were.

Just what I said. He had Brussels sprouts and carrots and I think a piece of turnip.'

'Yuk! Turnip and Brussels sprouts. That's disgusting,' they all chorused.

The children of Springfield were no different than any other children. They loved cakes and sweet things and only ate their vegetables under threat. They had never heard the word 'vegetarian' and would have had no idea what it meant. If asked, they probably would have guessed that a vegetarian was someone who lived in a place called Veggieland.

'You're making that up!' shouted Bob, who was one of the older boys.

'No, really, I'm not. It's true; I swear,' cried Joe, crossing his heart.

'Yeh, and that story about him being kidnapped by the fairies was true too,' sneered Bob.

Joe shrugged. 'Well no, not really. But he did have vegetables for lunch.'

'Yeh, right! I'll bet he did, and tomorrow he'll probably have a whole cabbage with him.'

All the children laughed as Bob slapped Joe on the back and the group dispersed, leaving Joe to walk the rest of the way on his own.

Ned, totally oblivious to what was going on with Joe, was enjoying his walk home. Springfield School was well outside the village. It was situated between Springfield and the smaller village of Crawfordshill and served as a school for the children of both villages. The way home led him past a few farms and through a little wood before bringing him out at Agnes's cottage, which was on the outskirts of the village. Ned's walk from school was very solitary. As Ned had only arrived in the village the day before, he wasn't aware that the other children did not walk this way to and from school. It was in fact the most direct route to the village, but they were content to walk an extra mile in order to avoid Agnes and her math tests.

As he walked, Ned thought up sums in his head, and he also recited passages from Shakespeare. He looked down at the handful of flowers he had picked for his mum from the hedgerows. Ned was trying to remember the Latin name for daffodils when an aroma filled the air around him. Ned's mouth watered as he sniffed the air. Could he be correct? Was that the smell of cabbage boiling? Yes, he was sure of it. The delicious smell was coming from the cottage at the end of the path. (The smell was the other reason the children avoided the cottage. Although Ned found the smell delicious, most other children would have agreed that their fathers' sweaty socks had a more appetizing smell.)

Ned knew it was rude to disturb people when they were having their dinner, so he leant quietly on the cottage gate and savoured the air around him. Eventually the smell made him so hungry he couldn't linger any longer. Reluctantly, he shuffled away from the cottage and made his way home. It wasn't far from Agnes's cottage to his uncle's farm, so in less than fifteen minutes he was setting his books down on the kitchen table.

Ned's mum had left a glass of milk on the table for him, along with a few sticks of raw carrot and a chunk of shortbread. He was happily chomping at the last piece of carrot and working at his history homework when his mum came in carrying a pail of milk. She frowned as she looked at the piece of untouched shortbread.

Looking at Mrs. Kenny, it was hard to believe she had once been the prettiest girl in her village. She had a worn look about her which was the result of years of worry and stress. Ned's mum worried about everything. She worried about the cleanness of her house and the tidiness of her garden. She stressed over the quality of her cooking and baking. But most of all, she worried about what her neighbours thought of her and her family.

Although she had been sad to leave her old home, she welcomed their new start. She was tired of the looks and gossip concerning Ned's strange ways. Her husband had been no help; in her opinion he didn't understand, as she did, the importance of fitting in. He was always encouraging Ned to read, and he seemed to be more amused than shocked when Ned talked what she considered nonsense. Before they had moved, she had made it clear that things were going to be different. Ned sat through what he thought were hours of lectures in which his mum explained how she expected him to behave in their new home.

'Hi, love. How was school?'

'Fine, Mum. I knew the answers to all the questions the teacher asked.'

Mrs. Kenny frowned at her son. 'Did you make any friends?'

'Well, a boy called Joe sat with me at lunch.'

'That's good, Ned. Just remember not to do or say anything they would find unusual.'

'Okay, Mum.' Ned sighed and cradled his head in his hands.

'Ned, I know it's hard for you. But you really have to try and fit in. Remember, your dad and I really want you to have some friends here. It's important for boys of your age to have friends. I know you are a smart boy, but it really isn't normal the way you get on.'

'I know, Mum. I will try; I promise.'

Ned finished his homework and helped his mum set the table. When his dad and uncle came in from the fields, he was seated at the table with his face and hands washed waiting patiently for his dinner. Mrs. Kenny dished out the food, and Ned happily dug in to his potatoes.

'Eh, what's this!' shouted Mr. O'Gill, who was a bit hard of hearing but never admitted it. 'The boy doesn't have any meat! Give the boy some meat!'

'Ned doesn't eat meat, Uncle Jack,' explained Mr. Kenny.

'He doesn't eat meat! Well, I never heard the like of it. No wonder he's so scrawny. What age are you, boy?' bellowed Mr. O'Gill. He slapped Ned so hard on the back that the boy spat chunks of turnip over the table.

'I'm nine, Uncle Jack,' Ned spluttered.

'Nine! Well, I would have said you looked more like six or seven. Why, when I was nine I was almost as tall as my father and weighed ten stone. I was even able to plough two fields on my own. I bet you couldn't do that.' Mr. O'Gill thumped his chest to make his point.

Ned believed him, for even at sixty Mr. O'Gill was still a tall, strongly built man.

When Mrs. Kenny brought a large apple pie to the table for dessert, everyone but Ned accepted a piece.

'I guess you don't eat apples either,' Mr. O'Gill stated.

'I like apples; I just don't like desserts or sweet things.'

Mr. O'Gill turned to Ned's dad. 'Edward, there's something wrong with your boy. He needs to be taken in hand. Keep him home from school tomorrow and he can work with me on the farm. I'm slaughtering some pigs. If that doesn't make a man of him, I don't know what would.'

'I can't stay off school. I . . . I have homework to hand in,' stuttered Ned. He looked pleadingly at his dad.

Mr. O'Gill totally ignored Ned. 'I'm telling you, Edward, you have been too soft with the boy. No good ever came from letting children fill their heads with all the trash they read in books.'

Ned had just opened his mouth to give his uncle a piece of his mind when his mum quickly covered his mouth and practically dragged him off to bed. Ned was furious. Even though they were discussing him, his mum told him it was a conversation for the grown-ups.

Ned sat at the edge of his bed and hugged himself. He was seriously worried. Although Ned idolised his dad, he was aware of his father's faults. Mr. Kenny was a quiet, easy going man who never raised his voice and always tried his best not to get involved in fights or quarrels. Ned knew that his uncle was a very formidable man, and he didn't think that his father would dare to go against Mr. O'Gill. Ned was sure that if only he had been allowed to have his say, he would have been able to convince his uncle that school was the best thing for him. Sitting in the dark, Ned considered all his options. He decided that if he were pulled out of school, his only option would be to run away.

That night, he had a very restless sleep. His dreams were all confused, and although he dreamed of sums as usual, in this dream he kept getting them wrong. Once, he even dreamt he was wearing a dunce's hat.

The next morning, tired and bleary eyed, he went down for breakfast. Ned knew his dad and uncle were already up and out working on the farm, so he had come down prepared to go to school. He thought that by keeping quiet he could slip away before he was noticed. Unfortunately for him, his mum was busy working in the kitchen, so he had no alternative but to sit down to breakfast. As he was eating, his mum put his lunch bag on the table. Ned nearly choked on his milk.

'Am I going to school?'

'Yes, and you have your dad to thank for that.'

Ned grinned. He jumped from his seat and grabbed his books and his lunch, but his mum stopped him before he reached the door.

'Ned, you should know that this is only permitted if you start trying to fit in and learn to make some friends,' Mrs. Kenny explained.

'And if I don't?' Ned asked.

'Well, then we'll have no alternative but to put you to work on the farm.'

'Seriously?' Ned almost screamed the word.

'Yes. I have to admit, I agree with Uncle Jack. I think it would do you good to get your nose out of your books for a while, but your father really wants you to stay in school.'

Ned realised that his mum was far from happy. She was scrubbing the table so hard that she was almost boring a hole in it. So with a quick 'cheerio' and promise to himself that he was going to be especially nice to his dad, Ned ran all the way to school.

# Chapter Four
# Friends

Ned had been attending Springfield School for a few weeks and although he knew he was supposed to, he hadn't made any friends. For the first few days, he had tried to be friendly to the other children, but they really didn't have anything in common. The more he excelled in school, the less they wanted to talk with him. They felt he was just too weird to be friends with. To his schoolmates, it didn't seem normal that children should be so into their studies. Secretly, though, they were jealous that his schoolwork seemed easy for him.

It wasn't entirely their fault. Ned was stubborn, and the constant lectures from his mum and the jibes from his uncle annoyed him. He could have bridged a little of the gap by being less enthusiastic about his studies and joining in on a game or two, but he was a little hurt by the comments and sneers about his lunches, so he didn't bother.

On his second day at school, he felt a little uncomfortable with the crowd of children who gathered around him at lunch break. Ned couldn't help but hear the whispers concerning the contents of his lunch bag. His school fellows were all amazed that he had vegetables for lunch, and they laughed at him when he explained that he didn't like meat or sweet things. Even Jennie, the pretty redheaded girl who had been making eyes at him the day before, looked at him as though he had just grown another head.

He had hoped that by the third day the other children would have gotten over their aversion to his choice of diet, but they hadn't, and he was bombarded by shouts of 'What do you have for lunch today, last night's potatoes?' Or 'We have some grass here, would you like some?' Ned was angry, but there was no way he was going to let them know, so he punished them by being an excellent student. On lunch, he made sure he sat far away from all the others.

Jennie, who had been seriously disappointed that Ned wasn't going to be her boyfriend, didn't miss an opportunity to tease him. She got more and more frustrated as Ned ignored her taunts. Jennie liked to be popular, and because of her looks she was. All the girls wanted to be her friend, and all the boys turned to mush when she batted her eyelashes at them. Not to be beaten, one day Jennie insisted that all the children had to stop speaking to Ned. Because of her popularity, they did. Ned wasn't too upset, as at least the taunts over his lunch stopped, but he never let his mum know. As far as she was concerned, he was friends with Joe.

Ned didn't feel lonely. He enjoyed living in his own little world with his books and dreams. Also, there was the cottage at the end of the lane. It still intrigued Ned. Each time he passed, the delicious aroma of vegetables cooking enticed him to go in. He never saw anyone around the house, but as the vegetable beds were neatly kept, Ned knew that someone must live there. As he loitered in the lane by the cottage, he imagined the type of person who lived there. He hoped that one day he would find out who really did live there.

One afternoon as he walked home, he was feeling exceptionally miserable. School had been particularly boring. They were learning about Elizabeth the First. Ned knew all about her, and as they were made to put their slates away so they could listen to their teacher, he couldn't even set himself sums. He was reciting Tennyson's *Charge of the Light Brigade* in an attempt to cheer himself up. Ned had just gotten to the line, 'Boldly they rode and well,' when a goat popped its head up over the gate of Agnes's cottage. Ned patted the goat. He liked goats.

'What is twelve times seventy five?' asked a voice from nowhere.

'Nine hundred,' answered Ned confidently.

'That's very impressive,' said the voice. 'I have seen you before. You stop each day and look at my house.'

Ned looked around the garden and spotted a middle-aged lady picking peas at the far side of the garden. 'Sorry, I didn't mean to be rude. I'll get going.'

'No, it's fine. In fact, why don't you come in? My name is Agnes, and I was just about to make some ginger tea. Would you like a cup?'

Ginger tea! Even the words made Ned's mouth water. While Agnes made tea, she fired sums, history questions, and spelling tests at him. Ned had never had so much fun in all his life. He felt very much at home in Agnes's cottage. She had a mountain of books in her parlour, and as she had only a few shelves, most of them were stacked up in orderly piles on the floor. Apart from these, she didn't have anything much of interest. Everything else she owned was of a practical nature. Ned thumbed through some of the books while she continued questioning him. He had just lifted Homer's *Odyssey* when Agnes came into the room carrying the tea tray.

'You can borrow that if you like,' she said.

'Can I really?'

'Yes. But only if you look after it and return it after you have read it.'

Ned clutched the book to his chest, 'I promise. Thank you.'

Agnes smiled; she really liked this boy, for he was very different from the other children of the village. For a start, he didn't run from her. More than that, he seemed to really enjoy being quizzed. The harder the questions, the more he seemed to like them. Ned sipped the tea, and he marvelled at how wonderful it was. They spent an enjoyable afternoon discussing books and history. Agnes was impressed by how knowledgeable Ned was, and Ned was pleased that Agnes listened and even agreed with his ideas and thoughts.

'That was really lovely,' he said as he drained his cup. 'I really should be getting home. My mum will be wondering what's keeping me.'

'I understand. I hope you will come back and visit me again,' said Agnes.

'Sure I will. Can I come back tomorrow?' Ned asked as he lifted his belongings.

'Of course, but only if you let your mum know. I wouldn't want her to worry,' answered Agnes.

Ned walked away from the cottage feeling happier than he had since he arrived at Springfield. He had never minded not having any friends, mainly because he had never met anyone who shared his interests. Now he had met Agnes, he realised what he had been missing.

Although Agnes was used to being alone, she couldn't help but feel that her cottage was a lot quieter and lonelier after Ned left. She looked forward to his next visit probably more than Ned.

Agnes realised that she had not explained to Ned while they were talking that she was a witch. All that evening she worried that Ned might find out about her from his family and that he might not be allowed—or worse, that he might not want—to come and visit with her again. That night, for the first time in her life, she was tempted to use her crystal ball to see what was going on in Ned's home, but she resigned herself instead to a restless, worrisome night.

Ned kept to his word and visited Agnes the very next day. She had spent the afternoon walking back and forward from the window in case she might miss him. When he appeared at her gate, it took all of her self-control not to run down the path to greet him. He was the first friend she had made in a very long time. Being a witch really killed your social life. Even when she was at school, her fellow students had avoided her, half of the children worried that she wouldn't like them and would decide to try out some of her nastier spells on them. The other half, meaning the boys, were eager to stay out of her way in case she doped them with a love potion.

Agnes had brewed some of her special dandelion tea and made some sprout and whole-wheat sandwiches. Ned thought they were delicious. He ate four and still wanted more, but he was too polite to ask. The previous night he had stayed up well past his bedtime reading the book Agnes had lent him. They spent some time talking about the book before Ned had to leave.

Much to Agnes's relief, Ned wasn't scared or put off when she explained that she was a witch. Instead, he was intrigued and would have asked her endless questions if she hadn't firmly changed the subject. Ned realised that Agnes wasn't comfortable with his questions and dropped the subject for what he thought was forever.

As the weeks went past, there wasn't a day when Ned didn't call with Agnes. He hadn't told his mum where he was going, only that he had made a friend and was spending time with his chum after school. Mrs. Kenny was so pleased that she didn't enquire further for fear of putting him off.

Although Ned and Agnes had long debates, they never talked of anything other than books and math, or occasionally history. Therefore, even after weeks of acquaintance they knew very little about each other. Agnes did wonder why Ned chose to spend his time with her instead of playing with his friends, but she was never one to pry. After all, she didn't like being quizzed about her past.

'Agnes, you know so much more than my teacher. Thanks for letting me come here every day,' said Ned out of the blue one afternoon.

He had just had another boring day at school; his teacher had given them all a new book to read, *Pilgrim's Progress*. Ned had read the book when he was seven, and he was frustrated that he was being kept back by the other children in his class.

'You don't need to thank me, Ned,' answered Agnes. 'I enjoy having you here. Did you have a bad day at school?'

Then it all came out. Ned explained how he didn't have any friends and how the children thought he was strange because of his diet or because he knew so much more than they did. He also told Agnes that he didn't really mind not having friends, but he explained that his mum was concerned and that he was worried that she would find out. Agnes looked at his serious little face and felt closer to him than she had before. He was so like her; they were two people who didn't really fit in.

'Agnes, I have to tell you something. My mum doesn't know I come here every day. I lied to her. I told her that I go to a school friend's house. It was the only way I would still be able to go to school. I want to go to university because I want to become a barrister, so, you see, I have to stay at school. I know I haven't been entirely honest, but when you think about it, I haven't been really lying. After all, you are my friend,' Ned blurted out.

'Ned, I am your friend. Although I am sorry you feel you can't tell your parents the truth.'

'You won't stop me from visiting, will you?' Ned asked. He tried to keep the concern from his voice but was unsuccessful.

'Of course I won't. I haven't been altogether truthful to my mother, either.'

Ned stared at Agnes. An adult admitting to telling a lie was new to him. He had caught adults out on a lie many times, but getting them to admit it, especially to a child, was a miracle Ned had never before experienced.

'You see, Ned, my mother is a very powerful and respected witch, and I can't tell her what a failure I am. She believes I am honoured by the people of Springfield. If she knew the truth, she'd be down here like a shot, getting in my way and meddling in my life.

'I do feel bad about lying to her, mainly because I'm scared of her finding out. She lives so far away that I just hope she'll never hear anything to the contrary. But that means I have to keep coming up with new reasons why she can't come to stay. I don't really mind. She may be my mother, but she is so interfering and domineering that I don't mind not seeing her.' Agnes chuckled.

'Seriously, Ned, it's wrong to tell lies, but I know it's also hard to pretend to be something you're not. You may not make many friends, but when you do you'll know they love you for what you are. But don't be too severe on your schoolmates. They haven't met anyone like you before. Just be patient and kind and keep trying to be friends with them. You never know; it might be worth it.'

'I'm not sure about that,' answered Ned.

'Well, we have to live in hope. At least, that's what I'm still trying to do.'

'Did you always want to be a witch?'

Agnes was quiet for a while before she answered. 'Well, because I'm being honest, I would have to say no. You see, I always wanted to be a teacher. I really love children, but I don't think they like me too much. But when you are a witch, you can't fly in the face of destiny. I have learned that the hard way. I wouldn't want you to have to give up school and your dream of becoming a barrister, so I won't let anyone find out you come here. But if you are found out, I'll try and find a way to teach you myself so you can still go on to university.'

'I wish you could be my teacher now. Miss Meek will never get me ready for the entrance exam,' Ned complained.

'What would you say if I tutored you outside school so you'll be ready for your university entrance exam?' Agnes asked.

'Do you mean it? You could be my teacher. You would be a great teacher; you know so much better than Miss Meek,' Ned said with great enthusiasm. 'It would be like having both our dreams come true.'

Agnes looked at Ned. He was right; it was her dream coming true, almost. She wasn't really doing anything wrong; after all, no one in Springfield used her services as a witch, so she may as well do as she pleased. So when Ned arrived from school the next day, Agnes had a study plan all laid out for him. Over a cup of mint tea and a few parsnip bakes, Agnes and Ned started organising his new curriculum.

# Chapter Five
# A New Witch

For Ned, the next few months were happy both at home and at school. His mum was pleased because he had made a good friend. Also, as he had started tending to the vegetable plot, his uncle was appeased and no longer talked about him coming out of school. Uncle Jack had even commented that the fresh air was doing Ned a world of good; he looked much healthier and had even put on some weight. To his surprise, Ned found that he really enjoyed working in the garden and had even made some improvements to the vegetable plot. It was now much bigger and tidier than it ever had been, and thanks to Agnes he had now a very impressive herb garden.

After a while the children in school seemed to have gotten used to him and were no longer as jealous as they had been when he first joined the school. They soon got bored with not talking to him, and although they weren't friends, he certainly wasn't treated as an outsider.

Then one day Joe had discovered that Ned was better at explaining sums than Miss Meek and had asked for his help with a maths test. When it got around that Ned had been instrumental in getting Joe a B in the test, Ned found himself surrounded by children all needing his help. So each lunch hour he held little classes to teach fractions and algebra. Miss Meek was impressed that her class was doing so well, but of course she credited her own teaching abilities and never once realised that Ned was solely responsible for the class's academic achievements.

As Ned sat eating his lunch one day in early June, his attention was diverted from the class he was teaching. Jennie was telling the other children about a new witch who had just moved to Springfield.

'But we have Agnes. We don't need another witch,' stated Ned as he put down his slate and joined the conversation.

'Well, Agnes isn't a proper witch. Everyone knows that. This one lives in a pretty cottage with flowers and cute little garden ornaments. Even my mum says Marie is really beautiful; she's like something out of a fairy tale, and when you pass her house all you can hear is her singing. She has such a beautiful voice. I'm going to visit her after school. My mum said I could.' Jennie was putting on her pompous voice, which Ned found irritating.

'Well, I don't want to meet her. She sounds peculiar,' mumbled Ned.

'Look who's talking about being peculiar,' sneered Jennie.

Ned didn't even bother retaliating. He just walked away as Jennie and her friends giggled.

Sitting in Agnes's cottage later that day, Ned was finding it difficult to concentrate. Questions he would normally have answered correctly he got dreadfully wrong.

'Ned, what is wrong with you today?' Agnes asked. He knew she was disappointed with him but was trying not to show it.

'Did you know another witch moved here?' Ned said as quietly as he could.

The cup Agnes was holding fell and smashed on the tiled floor, but she ignored it.

'Really? I didn't hear that. How are the villagers taking to her?' Agnes's voice was strangely flat.

'You know what they're like, Agnes. They don't appreciate a talented witch when they see one.' Ned hated himself for telling her, but he knew it was better that she hear it from him.

'So what you mean is they like her,' said Agnes.

Ned had started clearing up the broken teacup. It made him feel slightly more comfortable having something to do while Agnes was pacing the kitchen.

'Well, they think they do. But after all, she has only just arrived, so how can they really know?'

'Do you think they'll make me leave?' The concern in Agnes's voice was unmistakable.

Ned felt uncomfortable; he didn't know the answer to that question. It was something which had worried him all afternoon. Not that they would send her away but that she would feel compelled to leave.

'No, I don't think so. You wouldn't go, would you?'

Agnes sat down on the chair next to Ned and buried her face in her hands. Was she going to cry? Ned hoped not. He hated to see grownups cry. Agnes lifted her head and smiled weakly at him. There was no sign of tears, but there was sadness in her face.

'I guess I've always expected this; I just didn't think it would happen so soon. But . . . no. I won't leave—that is, unless they force me out. I have your education to consider, after all. Now pack up your books; it's time you went home. Don't forget, the essay on Cromwell is due tomorrow.'

Ned packed his books. He hesitated as he placed his hand on the doorknob.

'Agnes, I'm so sorry. I didn't want to tell you, but I thought I should before you heard it from someone else.'

'Don't you worry. I'm glad you told me. Now off you go and don't think anymore about it.'

That was easier said than done. Ned felt extremely miserable as he trudged home. There was only one thing for it: He would go and see what this new witch was like. He knew where she was living; Jennie had been pretty precise in her directions. Maybe if she was truly a good witch, she could think of some way they could help Agnes.

After Ned left, Agnes sat at the table and thought over the situation. She had known there was something wrong. Over the last few days, she had felt a change in the magic all around her. What was annoying her was that it had never occurred to her that another witch might have moved into the village. Agnes looked out into her garden; it would be a nice evening to go for a walk. And if her walk led her past this new witch's cottage, then all the better.

Ned's mum hadn't been too happy about letting him go out after dinner, but thanks to Uncle Jack intervening and accusing her of mollycoddling, Ned was soon walking down the winding track which would eventually lead him to Marie's cottage. He wasn't sure what to expect. If Jennie was to be believed, Marie was more like a princess from a fairy tale than a witch. As long as she didn't sing at him, he was sure he would be alright.

Unlike Ned, Agnes didn't have any idea where this new witch lived, and she had no intention of asking the villagers for directions. She had no alternative but to follow the waves of magic. Before long, she was sure she was on the right track. As she walked, she felt the magic growing stronger. Agnes tried to ignore the sinking feeling in her stomach. This witch's magic certainly felt stronger than hers. If it came to a standoff, she didn't think she had a chance.

As Agnes and Ned were making their way to her home, Marie decided she would head out for a walk herself. Before leaving, she had put some baking into the oven, and before long the enticing smell of fresh bread and cakes filled the air around her cottage. A couple out on an evening walk breathed in the delicious aroma. They smiled at each other. This was certainly better than the stench of boiling vegetables they were used to smelling around Agnes's cottage.

When Ned neared his destination, he wandered off the path. As the cottage came into view, he hid behind an oak tree. Looking at Marie's cottage, he couldn't believe his eyes. Although he lived in the countryside and was used to the pretty cottages and gardens, he had never seen anything like this before. Roses and honeysuckle smothered the walls of the cottage, and some had even managed to creep over the thatched roof. Pretty green shutters framed the sparkling windows. The front door was also painted green, and the paint was so shiny and new that it glinted in the evening sun.

The garden which surrounded the cottage was a mass of colour. Every flower imaginable grew in the beds. The brick path was almost covered with nasturtiums falling over a border of shells. Bay trees and standard roses flanked the path, and fully grown apple trees spread their branches over the edges of the garden. Here and there statues of brightly coloured garden gnomes, fairies, and animals littered the flower beds.

As Ned stared at the garden, he was surprised to see baby rabbits hopping through the flowers. His surprise was not because there were rabbits in the garden; it was due to the fact they weren't eating any of the abundance of flowers. In one corner, a tiny, unfettered lamb was lying under one of the apple trees. Two kittens frolicked on the terrace in front of the house, and on one of the windows ledges a large fluffy white cat lay licking its paws. Ned pinched himself to make sure he was awake, especially when he saw that the kittens were totally ignoring the flock of swallows which was swooping in and out of the garden. The barking of a dog drew Ned's attention away from the cottage, and that was when he saw Marie.

The most beautiful girl he had ever seen was walking from the wood towards the cottage. A small, awfully cute fox terrier pranced around her bare feet. Ned knew in his heart that this was Marie. She was no more than twenty. Her tiny, heart-shaped face was framed with the longest, blondest hair he had ever seen. Even from a distance he could see that her features were delicate, her eyes were the brightest blue, and her lips were full and red. Her figure was slight and elegant, and although she was wearing a simple white muslin dress, she was regal enough to be confused with a princess. She wore no jewellery except a large, ugly bloodstone ring which looked out of place on her dainty white hand. As Marie walked, she sang. Ned felt warm and happy inside as he listened to her voice.

Although Ned was more interested in his books than girls, he could feel the draw of the witch. Ned understood Jennie's infatuation with Marie. All the girls would want to be her, while all the boys would be falling madly in love with her. He suddenly felt shy; there was no way he could approach someone like Marie. With a sinking feeling he was aware that Agnes could never compete with her. Even though Agnes had lived in the village for years, he knew instinctively that the villagers would choose this new witch over her. He was just walking away when he saw a figure moving through the trees beside the witch's garden. Although he had just glimpsed it, he was sure it was Agnes, and he immediately felt guilty that he had been so enchanted by Marie.

Agnes had observed all that Ned had. She looked down at her plain, drab brown dress and all at once felt old and ugly. This new witch deserved to be Springfield's witch. Even if Agnes had not felt the power of Marie's magic, just one look at her would have been enough to convince Agnes of this. As Agnes walked away, the only hope left in her heart was that she would be allowed to stay in the village. Since she met Ned, she had found some purpose in her life.

# Chapter Six
## An Unwelcome Visit

Several weeks after Marie had moved to Springfield, Agnes was busy weeding her cabbage patch. It usually helped to lift her mood, but unfortunately it wasn't working this time. Her thoughts kept returning to Marie. Agnes had been finding it difficult to act unconcerned as she sat by and watched Marie getting accepted into Springfield. Marie had certainly won over the village, and except for Ned everyone raved about her. Marie had a constant string of villagers visiting her for cures and fortune telling. They thought she was a marvel.

Even the children loved her. As Agnes sat in church she couldn't help but overhear as they talked about playing in Marie's garden. It was a fairyland to them, and now that school had stopped for the summer they spent most of their time there. They loved everything from the beautiful flowers to the playful animals, and of course all the cakes and buns Marie constantly fed them didn't hurt her popularity.

Jealousy was eating away at Agnes. She was aware her feelings were ridiculous and childish. But she reckoned a little childishness never did anyone much harm. She had just finished scattering the cabbage patch with her homemade slug pellets when some visitors arrived.

Ten minutes later, a group of the most prominent villagers were sitting in Agnes's parlour. They were all looking very uncomfortable, including Agnes. She didn't need to be able to read the future to tell that this was not a social call. The villagers glanced at one another, willing someone to speak. Agnes sat stiffly with her hands clasped on her knees and her ankles crossed. Her eyes were lowered, and her lips were pursed. Her distant and prudish demeanour only added to the villagers' conviction they were doing the right thing.

If Ned had have been there, he would have been surprised and annoyed to see that his Uncle Jack made up one of the party. In fact, as the owner of the largest farm in the area, he had been behind the decision to approach Agnes. The tension in the room was so strong that when Mr. O'Gill cleared his throat to speak, some of the villagers actually jumped.

'Agnes, as you know, you came here seven years ago to be our village witch,' stated Mr. O'Gill rather loudly, as usual. Agnes nodded in agreement. 'And you also know that didn't work out the way we had all hoped. Since then, you have been living here with no real purpose.'

'Well, that's not technically true, Mr. O'Gill,' interrupted Agnes. 'I have still been making my potions, and in fact I have had the time to come up with some new, and if I may say so, extremely effective remedies. My chilli and poppy seed ear drops would really help with your hearing difficulty.'

'How dare you, Madam! I can hear a pin drop two rooms away,' bellowed Mr. O'Gill.

Agnes, unaware that it would have been better if she stopped speaking, went on.

'And you should really try my haemorrhoid cream, Miss Robinson. I know it would bring you great relief,' she said to a particularly cross-looking elderly lady.

'Impertinence,' snorted Miss Robinson as she adjusted the cushion she was sitting on.

It was well known that Miss Robinson had haemorrhoids; she even carried a soft, plump cushion with her in case she had to sit down. But she would never admit to having them. It was just something decent people didn't speak about. She was constantly in pain, and it made her very short tempered, so even the bravest of men wouldn't cross her. Only the children dared to make fun of her, but only when they were sure she wasn't around.

'We're getting away from why we came here,' reminded Mr. Bradley, the owner of the local pub. He was an enormous fat man who loved his food, but the smell of Agnes's turnip and broad bean soup was beginning to make him feel sick.

'Yes, quite,' shouted Mr. O'Gill. 'What we came to say was that if you feel the need to move to another village, we won't stand in your way. After all, there must be some place where you would feel more at home.'

'I understand what you are saying, Mr. O'Gill. But I have no inclination to leave Springfield. It's my home; there is nowhere else I want to be.'

It was a straightforward and simple answer but not the one they had been expecting and hoping for. Everyone sat in silence, not even daring to breathe. It was so quiet that if Mr. O'Gill could hear as well as he thought he could, he would indeed have been able hear a pin drop two rooms away.

'No, Agnes, I don't think you do understand us.' Miss Robinson's snide voice broke the silence. 'We are telling you to leave Springfield.' Miss Robinson took great delight in being the one to inform Agnes that she had to leave. She had taken the mention of her haemorrhoids very personally.

Mr. Bradley ran his finger around his collar; he was beginning to sweat. He had a feeling things were going to get ugly. Whether or not they accepted it, the fact was that Agnes was a witch, and you didn't go about pushing them around. Well, not if you wanted to wake up the next morning still human. They all watched Agnes, waiting for her to explode. When Agnes stood up, Mr. Bradley actually screamed and leaned so far back in his seat that he fell on the floor. Mr. O'Gill rolled his eyes as Mr. Bradley tried to heave his great bulk off the floor.

'Well, thank you for being so direct, Miss Robinson. I will make arrangements directly and will be on my way as soon as I can.' Agnes walked to the door and opened it for her guests.

The villagers didn't need to be told to leave; they were out of the cottage in a flash. As they got nearer to the village, their confidence increased.

'Are we sure she's a real witch?' Miss Robinson enquired.

'Well, if she is, that's the most pathetic excuse for one I have ever seen,' barked Mr. O'Gill.

'If I'd have known getting rid of her would have been so easy, I'd have done it ages ago,' said Miss

Robinson, her face contorting in to the closest it ever came to a smile.

After they left, Agnes sat on the floor by her front door and cried for the third time in her life.

# Chapter Seven
# Ned Has a Solution

When Ned walked into Agnes's home later that day, he was startled to find the cottage in a mess. Agnes's books and few belongings were piled up in the middle of the floor in the parlour, and a burning smell was coming from a pot on the stove. Lifting the lid, Ned saw that Agnes had let the soup boil dry. Ned was worried; Agnes was nowhere to be seen. It was so unlike her; she was normally so careful. She would never have left a pot on the stove unattended. She was also never away from home when he was expected.

Ned was about to go looking for her when Agnes came in through the back door. Her mousey brown hair, which was normally so neat, was hanging in untidy strands over her face.

'Agnes, what's wrong? Did someone hurt you?' yelled Ned, pushing forward a chair so she could sit down.

'Ned, what are you doing here?'

'I'm here for my lesson, Agnes . . . remember?' Ned was really worried now.

'Sorry, Ned. I didn't realise what time it was. But I can't tutor you today. I have to pack up my things and find somewhere new to live.'

'What?' Ned cried. 'You promised you weren't going to leave. I don't want to live here if you're not here.'

Agnes studied Ned, and for the first time since the villagers had left, she felt sorry for someone apart from herself. She sat down in the chair he had pulled out for her.

'I'm sorry, Ned. I had a visit today from some village representatives; they explained I had to leave Springfield.'

'And you agreed?' Ned couldn't believe what he was hearing.

'I . . . I didn't want to cause any trouble, and I don't want to live somewhere I'm not wanted,' explained Agnes.

'They never wanted you before, so why give in now?' Ned instantly wanted to take his words back. He couldn't miss the hurt as it flashed across Agnes's face. 'Sorry, Agnes. I didn't mean that. I'm just being selfish.'

'Don't apologise. It's true, after all. I have always known they didn't want me here, but they never came and said it to my face before. I can't ignore the wishes of the village.'

Ned muttered, 'But I don't want you to go.'

'I don't want to go either, but I have to. You must see that.'

Ned sat across from Agnes and looked as gloomy as he felt. Even her offer of dandelion tea didn't raise his spirits.

'Where are you going?' he asked finally.

'I don't know. I'll have to find somewhere soon. All I know is that I can't go back to my mother. She would be so disappointed. I couldn't do that to her—or to myself.'

Agnes got up and emptied out the burnt remains of her soup. She was just washing out the pot when Ned suddenly brightened up.

'Agnes, what if you could stay? You could live near the village but not in it.'

Agnes looked up from the pot. 'What do you mean?'

'Well, there's a deserted cottage not far from the school. I found it one day when I was having a walk. It would probably need a lot of work, but I could help with that,' explained Ned.

'Mmm,' said Agnes. She was trying not to get her hopes up. 'Your school is outside the village boundaries, isn't it?'

'Yes, and it's not in Crawfordshill's boundaries either. It's a sort of no man's land. So no one would be able to make you leave if you lived there.'

'Can you show me this cottage?'

She left the pot, grabbed her shawl, and took Ned's hand, and they both hurried off to look over what might be her new home. When Agnes returned, she was a lot happier. Ned was right; the cottage did need work, but she didn't mind that. Ned had also found out from a worker at a neighbouring farm that the cottage had been empty for a very long time. It had once been owned by a witch who had turned bad, and because of that no one had dared to live there. It was perfect, and it meant that she could stay near Ned.

A few days later, Miss Robinson took it upon herself to call at Agnes's cottage. When she saw that the vegetables had all been dug up from the garden, she smiled her little wry smile. Miss Robinson wanted to be completely sure Agnes had gone, so she pushed open the gate and walked up the path. Simply out of habit, she knocked on the front door. When she received no answer, she crept around to the front window and peered into the parlour. Miss Robinson almost squealed with delight when she observed the bare room. It didn't take her long to spread the good news that Agnes had left around the village.

# Chapter Eight
## Where's Jennie?

Summer had drawn to a close, and so had September, before Agnes finally felt that her cottage was completed to her standard. She knew that it would have taken a lot longer if Ned had not visited every day to help her. The interior had taken quite some time to get in order. The kitchen especially had posed quite a challenge. But that was nothing compared to the garden. Agnes had dug up all her vegetables and had brought them with her. But as it had taken so long to 'weed out the weeds,' some of the vegetables had withered and died long before she was ready to plant them.

It was fortunate that she had made some preserves and also that Ned had been able to bring her some fresh vegetables from his own garden, so she had enough to live on for the summer months.

The residents of Springfield had no idea where she had moved to, and she was determined to keep it that way, so appearing in the local market to buy greens would not have been a good idea.

When school started again, the children insisted that Ned start his lunchtime classes again; they were the only thing which made the long, dreary school day tolerable. Ned realised he had definitely learnt all he could from his country school mistress. Even so, day after day he faithfully attended. It was true that he did watch the clock and spent most of his time wishing the day away. But it was something his teacher was not aware of. To Miss Meek, Ned was a model pupil. He was always top of the class in tests. His compositions were without fault, and his homework was never tardy.

One Monday morning, Jennie didn't appear at school. Ned didn't find this out of the ordinary. Most of the children took days off here and there, either due to sickness or so they could help around their homes or farms. It wasn't until he heard her friends whispering at lunch that he became intrigued about why she wasn't in school. Lucy, Jennie's closest friend, was clearly upset over Jennie's absence, and some of her other friends were attempting to console her as she cried.

'Joe, what is the matter with Lucy?' asked Ned as Joe walked past him.

'Didn't you hear?' Joe sat on the bench beside Ned. 'Jennie never arrived home from school last Friday. No one has seen her all weekend. Her mum is hysterical.'

'Has no one looked for her?' asked Ned.

'Yes, her dad and some of the men in the village have been looking all weekend. But there's been no sign of her. Not even a dropped handkerchief,' answered Joe.

'Who was the last person to see her?'

'Lucy. That's why she's so upset,' explained Joe. 'They had a bit of a falling out, and Lucy stormed off with some other girls, leaving Jennie to walk home on her own.'

'Where did all that happen?' Ned asked.

'She was last seen at the crossroads outside the village. They reckon she went off with someone. They're saying it was a gypsy. There is a camp a few miles from here. Her dad went out to their camp, but he found nothing there.'

Jennie was not a particularly bright girl, but she wouldn't have been stupid enough to go off with someone she didn't know. Also, Jennie was a bit of a snob, so Ned knew there was no way she would have gone off with a gypsy. If she went off with someone, it would have been with someone of quality—but there was no one like that living anywhere near Springfield.

'I don't believe she went off with a gypsy,' Ned observed.

'No, neither do I,' agreed Joe. 'Everyone is being so stupid. In fact, I think I know where she went.'

'Where do you think she went?' asked Ned. He didn't believe that Joe knew anything, but he liked Joe and didn't mind humouring him.

'I can't say without proof. But after school I'm going investigating,' said Joe with a wink.

'Joe, you will be careful, won't you?'

'Sure I will. But I'm not a soppy girl, and I'm bringing Billy with me. No one will touch me when he's around, and when I rescue Jennie I'll be a hero.'

Ned watched Joe as he walked away. Even though Jennie could be annoying, he didn't like to think of one of his schoolmates going missing, and he hoped that she would be found unharmed.

The Billy Joe was speaking about was the stray dog that had lived in and around the village since he was a puppy. No one was sure where he had come from; he just seemed to appear one day. He was certainly a mongrel and was so mismatched that it was evident that he had come from a long line of mongrels.

Billy was a nuisance; he stole food from every house and cottage within a two-mile radius of the village. But apart from his unfortunate tendency towards participating in the occasional act of theft, he was a very good, loyal dog. The Springfield children loved him as much as he loved them. Although he was a stray, he was certainly not homeless. His normal practice was to move around the homes of all the children. Apparently it was Joe's turn to have him to visit.

While Ned and Joe were discussing Jennie's disappearance, Billy, who had been chasing birds in the wood, was conscious of a rumbling in his stomach. It had been a few hours since his last good meal. Joe had fed him rather well on some leftover pork. He could definitely go for some more of that right now. But his doggy brain knew Joe wasn't going to be home from school for a few hours, and he wanted something to eat right away. Billy lifted his head and sniffed the air. There was something delicious cooking somewhere nearby. After a short run, he neared the source of the cooking; it was coming from a nearby cottage.

As he ran up the path to the cottage, he was aware of the flowers around him growing rapidly in size. When an extremely large bluebottle flew past him, Billy realised it wasn't the flowers growing. It was him shrinking! Suddenly, his legs seemed strangely stiff—so stiff, in fact, that he could no longer move. Billy attempted to open his mouth to bark, but his muzzle failed to move. It only took a few seconds for Billy to become as still as stone. Only his doggy brain remained active. As someone picked up his frozen form, he was wondering how an intelligent dog like him had got into this mess.

# Chapter Nine
## More Disappearances

The next morning Ned raced to school hoping to have a word with Joe before school started. He had discussed Jennie's disappearance with Agnes, and she agreed that the situation was worrying. As Agnes couldn't investigate, she had commissioned him with finding out all he could about the day Jennie disappeared. But as she felt it wasn't wise for him to go off investigating on his own, she made it clear that he was simply to pick up what he could from the children at school and from anything he heard at home.

Ned waited outside the school for a long time, but there was no sign of Joe. When Miss Meek ordered him inside, he had no alternative but to obey her. Halfway through the morning, Mr. Mullen, Joe's father and the village blacksmith, came walking into the school room. He had the appearance of a man who had been up all night. After speaking with Miss Meek for a few moments, he addressed the class.

'Sorry for disrupting your studies, but our Joe didn't come home from school yesterday. I was wondering if he told any of you where he was intending to go.'

Gasps went around the room, and a few of the girls, including Lucy, started to cry. Ned was annoyed with them, but he sympathized with Mr. Mullen. The man was clearly upset; while he was talking, he was twisting his cap in his shaking hands.

Ned put his hand up. 'Mr. Mullen, Joe was speaking with me yesterday at lunch; he said he thought he knew where Jennie was. I think he was intending to go to find her.'

Mr. Mullen couldn't have looked more shocked. 'Did he say where he thought she was?'

'No, I'm sorry. I did ask him, but he wouldn't tell me. He said he didn't have proof.'

'Stupid boy. What was he thinking?'

'He said he was taking Billy with him,' Ned explained.

'Billy can't be found either.' Mr. Mullen wiped away his tears with his cap and walked out of the school room.

Agnes was clearly troubled when Ned told her about Joe. She warned him against investigating Joe's disappearance; she also made him promise that he would tell her before going anywhere other than her cottage, school, and home. She had even taken to walking him from her cottage and only let him stray from her side when his house was in view. Even then she stood watching him to make sure he made it through the door safely. Ned thought she was being a little too protective, but then more children went missing.

Lucy and some of her close friends were the next to disappear. Then Bob and a few of the older boys vanished one day after heading into the woods. Miss Meek was the first adult to disappear. When the children left her one afternoon, she was sitting at her desk grading papers. The next morning, the papers were there, but there was no sign of Miss Meek. Although many believed she had really just left the village because she was afraid, Agnes and Ned weren't so sure.

After Miss Meek, went missing the school was closed. The parents thought it was a good thing, as most of the children had disappeared on their way to or from school. All the children suddenly found themselves under constant supervision. Even Ned found himself under house arrest. Mrs. Kenny, still unaware where Ned really went after school, said Ned and his little friend would be safer staying in their own homes. Even when Ned begged and pleaded, she was firm in her decision. Even his Uncle Jack backed her up. Agnes missed her student but was relieved that Ned did not have to walk through the woods.

The next adult to go missing struck terror into hearts of all the residents of Springfield. Mr. Mullen had gone out one evening on his own looking for Joe. He had told no one what direction he was heading. The only thing his neighbour knew was that he had said he was going to check the only place they hadn't searched. Four days later, he had not returned. If Mr. Mullen could be taken, there was no hope for anyone. He was the biggest and bravest man in the village; it would have taken someone exceedingly formidable to overpower him.

After Mr. Mullen vanished, two more children were reported missing. Their parents were devastated; the twin girls had been playing in the garden behind their house. One minute they were there, and the next, they were gone. The men went out in groups looking for them. One group of men didn't return; six men vanished into thin air.

The villagers spoke of monsters, and a few were convinced the fairies were to blame. Some still blamed the gypsies, but when a band of men went to the camp to confront them, they found to their amazement that the gypsies had lost just as many as the villagers had. It didn't take long for people to start packing up and fleeing Springfield. Many of the houses and businesses were boarded up with no word of when their owners would return. It was a very sad sight.

# Chapter Ten
# Agnes Starts Investigating

Agnes went over in her head all the information Ned had been able to provide her with. True, it wasn't much, but she had a vague recollection that she had heard or read of something like this happening before. She just couldn't put her finger on it. She went through all her books and diaries for something which would give her some idea what was going on. Despite all that had happened, Agnes felt a strong responsibility for the people of Springfield. She was surprised that Marie hadn't stepped in to help. But she realised that it wasn't her place to criticize; after all, she wasn't in possession of all the facts.

After a week and four more disappearances, Agnes put aside the book she had been sifting through. There was nothing in it which was going to help. She had to use resources she normally wouldn't. Agnes opened the trunk which sat at the bottom of her bed. After rummaging for a few minutes, she produced a crystal ball. She set the ball on her kitchen table and grimaced as she stared into it. It wasn't that she couldn't use a crystal ball; she just didn't feel comfortable using it. The future was something she preferred to keep unknown.

Agnes concentrated and peered deeper into the depths of the ball. For a long time, there was nothing to see. Suddenly her eyes widened with shock. She ran to the kitchen cupboard, pulled out a large, dusty bottle, and with trembling hands poured herself a glass of blackcurrant wine. The image of what she had just seen stayed clear in her mind. She had wanted to see what had happened to those who had gone missing. But instead she saw that Ned was heading into danger. The trouble with looking into the future was that you didn't get a timeline. It could be happening tonight or in a month's time. Agnes knew she couldn't wait; she had to warn him straight away.

Winter had definitely come to Springfield. Agnes wrapped herself up in a heavy grey cloak and stepped into the frosty night. For the first time since she had left, she took the path which led to the village. She wasn't concerned with meeting anyone. She knew those left in the village were too afraid to leave their homes after dark. Agnes slipped quietly into the yard of Mr. O'Gill's farm. She could hear the murmur of voices in the parlour; she didn't stop to listen. Agnes knew that Ned would be tucked up in bed, so she crept around to the back of the house.

Ned had once told her that he slept in a room at the back of the old farmhouse. Agnes deduced that the window with the curtains drawn was Ned's room. She threw a handful of gravel at the window and hoped she was correct. After a moment or two, she saw the curtain twitch. Then Ned's face appeared at the window. He threw open the window and leant out.

'Agnes, what are you doing here?' whispered Ned.

'Ned, I need to warn you. I saw you in my crystal ball. You have to stay inside. Don't leave the house for any reason until I come for you.'

'How long for?' asked Ned.

'Until the person behind this is caught. Ned, I'm sorry that's all I can tell you, but you need to promise me you'll do as I ask,' Agnes pleaded.

'I promise, but I'm really bored, Agnes,' complained Ned.

'I thought you might be, so I brought you some books. I'll leave them beside the front door for you. Make sure someone is with you when you go to get them.'

Agnes waved at him and slipped around to the front of the house. She placed a posy of rosemary and lavender over the front door for protection before leaving the little pile of books. Ned lay back in his bed. He knew Agnes was just looking out for him, but he knew he could be useful to her if she just let him.

Flurries of early snow swirled around Agnes as she made her way back to her cottage. She usually loved the snow, but she barely noticed it now. The air around her became colder. A little shiver ran up her back, and the hairs on her arms stood on end. It was not the cold making her feel this way; it was the evil atmosphere around her. She had never felt anything so potent. Agnes heard the crack of a twig behind her. As she turned, a flash of blue light hit her in the face. She fell back unto the damp, leaf-covered path.

# Chapter Eleven
# Agnes in Trouble

Agnes awoke in the early hours of the morning. She was lying at the side of the snow-covered path. It took her a few moments to remember what had happened. She shook the covering of snow off her cloak and tried to wrap it tightly around herself, but it was too wet. Although she was sore and exhausted and had a splitting headache, Agnes managed to drag herself to her cottage. She changed her clothes and made herself a strong cup of ginger tea, adding some pepper as she couldn't chance falling sick with a cold.

As she sat at her table, she tried to put together her deductions. Her conclusions seemed impossible, but there was only one way to be sure. Could it be that Marie was behind all the disappearances? It seemed totally impossible, but it was the only conclusion which made any sense. After all, this nightmare had only started after she had arrived. But Agnes needed evidence, and she had no alternative; she had to search Marie's cottage. Maybe she was wrong, and Marie was in trouble; if she was, Agnes was prepared to do anything to help her. Agnes's cloak was still soaking from her night-time adventure. So she put on the heavy brown shawl she wore gardening before slipping out into the snow-kissed morning.

As she was tired, it took her longer to reach Marie's cottage than it had the last time she had come to spy. Also, this time she was being a lot more careful; she didn't want to be caught. If she was correct in her assumptions, there was something very evil lurking there. As Agnes neared the cottage, she secretly wished she had consulted her crystal ball. She might have been able to see if the cottage was empty. But it soon became evident that she didn't need to check the ball. Marie's singing was ringing out from inside the cottage. Agnes hid in the trees at the side of the cottage waiting for her opportunity.

As she waited, she tried to work out where all the missing people were being held. Agnes was sure they were still alive, but she wasn't sure what condition they were in. Her legs were stiff and she was shaking with the cold before she saw her chance. A rumble of voices startled the birds in the trees above her. Leaning forward Agnes saw Mr. O'Gill, along with four heavily armed men, approaching the cottage. She was deciding if she should stop them from entering when the door opened and Marie danced up the pathway.

'Hello,' said Marie, smiling. She did have a very becoming smile.

'Marie, I'm sorry for calling unannounced,' boomed Mr. O'Gill. 'But we really need your help with all these disappearances.'

'Thank you, Mr. O'Gill. I had been waiting and hoping you would let me help. I know I can, you know, but it was not my place to impose.'

'We were wondering if you would come with us. I have assembled all the people left in the village in the inn, and I would very much like for you to speak to them.'

'Certainly, Mr. O'Gill. Let me just get my cloak.'

It took Marie all of two minutes to get ready. Taking Mr. O'Gill's arm, she left with him for the village. Agnes didn't wait; she ran to the garden gate and carefully pushed it open. When Agnes saw the garden, she felt sick. She suddenly realised what had happened to the missing villagers. They had been transformed into little statues. The last time she had seen Marie's garden, there had been a quite a few ornaments littering the flowerbeds. But today the garden was literally packed with them. There were brightly coloured gnomes, impish fairies, and several startled-looking animals. Agnes grabbed the nearest gnome and ran out of the garden back into the woods.

She praised herself all the way home on her stealth. As it had started snowing again she knew her footprints wouldn't leave a trace. Unfortunately, Agnes hadn't noticed the bright-eyed blackbird watching her from one of the bare apple trees. As soon as she left, the bird flew into the air. A few moments later, it perched on Marie's shoulder and chirped in her ear.

'Do you understand what he's saying?' Mr. O'Gill enquired.

'I do. Every word,' Marie answered with a large smile.

When Agnes arrived home, she placed the chubby gnome on her kitchen table and proceeded to chant spells over it. An hour later, she still hadn't had any luck transforming the gnome. The urge to give up was tempting. She was sore, tired, and hungry. Deciding a break was just what she needed, Agnes ladled some sprout and spinach stew into a bowl and sat down for a bite to eat. Feeling full, she closed her eyes for a few moments to give them a rest. Five minutes later, she was snoring loudly. The person inside the gnome was trying to drone out the din by singing bar songs. It only wished it could do something about the smell of the stew.

Meanwhile, the residents of Springfield had sat quietly in the pub while Marie addressed them. When she had explained her conclusions, they got angry, and they showed their anger by shouting as loudly as they could. Mr. O'Gill, of course, shouted the loudest and it wasn't long before he had convinced the people they needed to take action. The mob nearly took the doors of the inn off their hinges as they exploded into the village square.

Anyone watching Marie would have been confused by the flash of triumph in her face. It had been easier than she thought. A bit of alcohol and a motivational speech were all it took to manipulate these people. Marie didn't even bother following the rabble; she knew she didn't need to. They would do what they had to without her.

Agnes was still fast asleep when the first blow struck her door. She was still not quite awake when the torch-bearing mob, brandishing pitchforks and sticks, smashed into her cottage. Before she knew what was happening, her hands were bound, and she was being dragged through the woods in the direction of the village.

The gnome on the kitchen table wondered how mobs always managed to find torches and pitchforks. Was there someone in every village who kept a shed full of them just in case they were ever needed?

# Chapter Twelve
# Ned in Danger

Before leaving the village for his farm, Mr. O'Gill had made sure that Agnes was securely imprisoned in the smithy. He had commissioned two men to guard her and had threatened them with slow and painful punishment if they allowed her to escape. Feeling as if he owned the world, he sauntered home.

Mr. O'Gill was oblivious to the upset he had caused at home. Mr. Kenny had been anxious. His uncle had left earlier in the day without any word of where he was going. When dinnertime came and his uncle had not yet returned, he had wondered if he should set out to look for him. Mrs. Kenny was frantic, and when her husband had suggested leaving to search for his uncle, she went into hysterics. So when Mr. O'Gill finally arrived home, Mrs. Kenny instantly annoyed him by bursting into tears.

'Give over crying, woman. Whatever is the matter with you?' Mr. O'Gill roared.

'Sorry, Uncle Jack. We thought you had been taken by the monster,' explained Mrs. Kenny through her sobs.

'Well, as you see, I'm fine, so stop blubbering and get me my dinner. Anyway, there'll be no more disappearances. We have caught the culprit and locked her in the smithy.'

They all stopped what they were doing and stared at him, even Ned, who had been engrossed in his book.

'Who was it, Uncle?'

'Agnes.'

'No, Uncle Jack, that's not true! It's not Agnes. She wouldn't do anything like that,' screamed

Ned, his book dropping to the floor as he jumped to his feet.

'Sit down, boy. You know nothing about it. You don't even know Agnes or what she is capable of. It seems that she didn't leave as quietly as we all thought. She has been living in a cottage near the school. She must have done this in revenge for us kicking her out,' Mr O'Gill explained.

'Near the school. Oh my goodness. That's horrible,' said Mrs. Kenny with a gasp.

'Where are all the people she took?' Mr. Kenny asked.

'We don't know. She is insisting she is innocent. But none of us believes her. Don't worry: we'll find out, and when we do, it'll be the rope for her.'

'No, you can't hang her. She's a good witch. I know she is! She's my friend!' Ned flew at his uncle, kicking and punching him. When his dad managed to drag him off his uncle, large tears were rolling down Ned's cheeks.

'I'm sorry, Uncle Jack. I don't know what has come over him. I'll take him to bed,' said Mr. Kenny.

'Don't apologise. It's the first sign he's shown of having a backbone. Although why he has taken sides with that witch is beyond me.'

Ned allowed his dad to carry him to bed. He didn't struggle at all. When his mum came up to him a few moments later, he didn't respond to her scolding. Later, as he lay staring into the blackness of the night, he realised that he had to do something to help Agnes. But he knew he couldn't do it on his own. Ned didn't sleep much that night, and when the first light broke into his room, he dressed and slipped out of the house. He walked past the smithy where he knew they were holding Agnes. Two men were still posted outside. His stomach lurched; he wasn't sure how long he had before they would hang her.

He ran all the way down the path out of the village and only stopped when he reached Marie's cottage. When he reached the cottage, he doubled in two, panting. Ned's glasses had steamed up with the heat of his face, so he didn't see the door opening, but he did feel sharp, claw-like fingers digging into his shoulders as he was pulled into the cottage. His feet didn't touch the ground as he as was flung across the room. He hit his head hard as he connected with the wall. For a long time, he was not aware of anything around him.

# Chapter Thirteen
# Agnes Takes Action

Agnes awoke a little while after Ned had. The smithy was cold and stank of horses. The furnace hadn't been lit since the disappearance of Mr. Mullen. It was not a very nice place to wake up in. In fact, it wasn't a nice place to go to sleep in. But as Agnes had been so exhausted from her ordeals that day and the previous night, her head had hardly touched the cold stone floor before she was fast asleep.

She pulled at the ropes restraining her hands; the damp had helped to loosen the knots. In a short time, she had managed to free herself. She crept to the door and quietly opened it just a crack. The men at the door were both sleeping. Agnes took her opportunity; she pushed open the door far enough for her to squeeze out. Running as fast as her legs would carry her, she sprinted across the village square into the surrounding wood. There was only one place she wanted to go to: Marie's cottage.

During her cold and uncomfortable sleep, Agnes had had a very strange dream. In her dream, she was just a little girl, and she was listening to a story. It was a story about the theft of a magical fairy amulet. As Agnes ran through the wood and down the path which would eventually bring her to Marie's cottage, she thought about her dream. She was sure her dream had been an old memory, but it was something more. It was magic, and the magic was showing her how to defeat the evil which had taken over the village. Agnes was worried. As we all know, being told how to do something and actually being able to do it are two very different things. Agnes, being extremely intelligent, knew this too.

All seemed quiet as Agnes approached the cottage. At first she wasn't sure if Marie was even there. When she heard Marie talking, she panicked. Perhaps she had been wrong and Marie wasn't working alone. Agnes faltered for a few minutes; she was unsure if she could defeat Marie, but she was certain that she couldn't defeat two enemies. She decided there was nothing for it; she had to find out what she was up against.

Very slowly and quietly, Agnes crept up the path and across the front of the cottage. Being careful not to be seen by those inside, she peered into the cottage. The room she was looking into was a very large kitchen. Marie was pacing around the room, and she was talking to herself! Agnes, who was too sensible to ever talk to herself, thought this was extremely odd. It was obvious that Marie was angry, and even worse than that, she was clearly insane. For a few moments Agnes felt sorry for her, but then she remembered her dream. Marie didn't exist at all; the spell was just a glamour hiding an evil, hideous monster.

Agnes almost fainted when she saw a large birdcage hanging from the ceiling. Something was curled up inside the cage, but it wasn't a bird; it was a boy. To Agnes's horror, she saw that it was Ned, and he wasn't moving. There was no time to lose; she had to face Marie.

While Agnes was creeping about outside her cottage, Marie was inside getting very angry. She hadn't expected Ned to turn up at her door; she hadn't even heard him as he came up the path. Marie had been less vigilant since Agnes had been captured. That morning she had even forgotten to put on her glamour. She had actually opened the door in her true form and found the boy there! Marie wasn't sure if he had seen her, as he had been bent over, but she couldn't take any risks. She had her glamour on now. When the boy awoke, she would know everything, so all she could do was wait. It was all so annoying. She couldn't curse him now that Agnes was in custody; she would have no one to blame it on.

'It's no use,' she said to herself. 'If he remembers, I'll have to wipe his memory and let him go. I hate that! I hate letting horrible children get away!'

At that point Agnes burst into the room and, catching Marie totally off guard, flung herself at the other witch, knocking them both to the floor. Agnes quickly pinned Marie down by the arms. Marie struggled against her before finally freeing her arm. As soon as she had, she aimed a curse straight at Agnes's chest. The curse wasn't strong enough to kill, but the force was enough to slam Agnes into the wall. The curse made Agnes's head fuzzy, but she was able to jump out of the way as Marie aimed another curse at her. The spell hit a vase of flowers which had been on the table beside her, and they exploded, sending water, glass, and scorched greenery around the room.

Agnes was quick to retaliate. A ball of white flame shot from her hand and pelted towards Marie. Marie darted out of the way but slipped slightly on the water from the vase. The ball of flame skimmed the edge of her skirt, setting it on fire. There was a scream of frustration from Marie before she directed the flames back at Agnes. They hit Agnes, only to be quenched by a shower of water which had magically sprung from her fingers.

Marie struck again. Red light streamed from her pointed finger, and the blackbird that had been perched on the windowsill transformed into an enormous crow. The crow flew straight at Agnes. As she brought her hands up to protect her face, the crow violently pecked at her. With her bleeding hands, Agnes swiped at the crow. With a lucky blow, she hit it out of her way. Without hesitating, she aimed a curse at it, freezing it in midair.

The two witches faced each other again, and at the same time light shot from their fingers. Green came from Marie's and sliver from Agnes's. The shawl Agnes was wearing transformed into a giant brown snake, which twisted itself around her neck and shoulders, pinning her arms to her sides. Fingers of ice spread over Marie's body, cracking as they wound their way around her arms, legs, and face. For a few moments, both the witches were held powerless by their trappings.

# Chapter Fourteen
## Mr. O'Gill Takes Action

Agnes had just disappeared through the trees at the far side of the square when Jimmy O'Loane opened his eyes and stared before him across the village square. He rubbed his eyes. He was cold, hungry, and miserable, and to top it off he had a blazing hangover. He poked at the embers of the dying fire, which only succeeded in putting it out completely. Jimmy reached into his coat and pulled out an almost-empty bottle of whiskey. With one large swig, he emptied the bottle.

Night watch at the smithy was, in his opinion, the worst job imaginable. He would have reconsidered if he had ever spoken with Hugh McPew, the drain cleaner for the Belfast Sewer System. Jimmy looked over to his friend Paddy. Paddy was fast asleep and snoring so loudly that

Jimmy was surprised he hadn't woken the entire village. Jimmy stood up, stretched, and kicked Paddy on the thigh.

'Get up, you lazy oaf. Mr. O'Gill will murder you if he catches you sleeping!' Jimmy shouted at his friend.

Paddy opened his eyes and smacked his lips. 'Sorry. Did I doze off?'

'You did. Just as well I was here to cover for you.' Jimmy didn't feel bad for deceiving his friend; he knew that if Paddy had woken first, he would have done the same thing.

'Better see how the old hag is, I guess,' said Paddy. He stood up and opened the door of the smithy. 'Here, Jimmy, you won't like this. The old hag's gone.'

'Gone! What do you mean gone?' shouted Jimmy in a panic. He pushed Paddy out of the way and stared into the empty smithy. 'Ooh, she's vanished. Mr. O'Gill won't be pleased.'

Mr O'Gill was just finishing his usual morning fry-up when Paddy and Jimmy burst into his kitchen. They had been quarrelling all the way to the farm about who was going to break the bad news to Mr. O'Gill. Neither of them wanted to face his wrath. But as they approached the farm, each realised that his own version of the story would be better, simply because he could divert the attention from his own incompetence.

'What's the meaning of this? And why are you not guarding the witch?' bellowed Mr. O'Gill.

'She . . . she's gone, sir,' stammered Jimmy

'Vanished into thin air,' whispered Paddy.

Mr. O'Gill, as they knew, did not have a sense of humour. 'If this is some kind of joke, I don't find it funny,' he said angrily.

'No, it's not, honestly. Come and see.' Paddy opened the door for Mr. O'Gill.

Mr. O'Gill followed the two men to the smithy. He occasionally shouted threats at the men, reminding them of what awaited them if they were playing some prank. When they arrived at the smithy and Mr. O'Gill saw that it was empty, he got even more furious.

'Did you two fall asleep and let her get past you?'

'No, sir. Honestly, we didn't,' said Paddy. Jimmy nodded in agreement.

'I don't believe you. Agnes couldn't just vanish. She's not witchy enough to do that!'

Paddy and Jimmy tried to look as innocent as they could. This was not easy, as they were both guilty. They were even too nervous to remind Mr. O'Gill that Agnes was witchy enough to abduct more than half the village. It didn't take long for Mr. O'Gill to round up the villagers. This time Mr. Kenny insisted on going too. They were just preparing to leave when Mrs. Kenny ran into the village square. She was wringing her hands and crying. When she reached Mr. Kenny, she grabbed his arm and screamed.

'Ned's missing. He's not in his bed, and he's nowhere around the farm.'

'That does it,' shouted Mr. O'Gill. 'She's gone too far this time! The nerve of her abducting my nephew! We need Marie. It's going to take a witch to catch a witch.'

Mr. O'Gill and his mob of villagers, this time minus the torches but still brandishing their pitchforks, marched in the direction of Marie's cottage.

They were just coming to the end of the woodland path when they heard the commotion. When they looked towards the cottage, they saw flashes of green, red, blue, and yellow light illuminating the windows. If any of them had ever been at a fireworks display, they would have thought Marie was having one in her cottage. But as they never had, they put it down to one thing: magic!

Any normal person would have walked away at this point, but curiosity is not only a failing of cats. The mob made its way up Marie's garden path and stopped at the window to spy. They saw Marie launching a spell at Agnes, turning her cloak into a snake. They were sure Agnes couldn't beat that. When they saw her counterspell of ice, their mouths fell open in amazement. Agnes was doing real magic . . . and she was good at it!

'Told you she vanished,' said Paddy as loudly as he could.

# Chapter Fifteen
## The Villagers Get a Shock

Agnes muttered a spell under her breath, and the snake which was coiled around her fell to the floor and turned back into her shawl. Meanwhile, the ice had completely covered Marie; suddenly, there was a loud crack, and pieces of ice shot off around the room. Some embedded in the walls, and a few catapulted through the windows. One narrowly missed Paddy, who failed to duck as quickly as the others.

Marie was shaking with anger while Agnes remained calm. Marie shot spells at Agnes in rapid succession. The first spell Agnes diverted with a shield of yellow light. The second missed its mark and hit the wall to the side of her head. Yellowish green ooze slid down the wall, burning a hole in the paint and plaster. The next curse was aimed low, and black tendrils grew from the stone floor and wrapped themselves around Agnes's legs, toppling her to the floor. She was still falling as the next spell came at her. Agnes raised an open hand, and a force of energy sent the spell bouncing back at Marie. She hadn't been expecting it, and a suffocating fog surrounded her. Marie choked as misty fingers wrapped themselves around her throat.

Agnes struggled against the tendrils as they tightened around her legs. She conjured a spray of salt, repelling the tendrils and forcing them back into the ground. Agnes grabbed the back of a chair and pulled herself to her feet. As she did so, she caught a glimpse of the villagers at the window. Marie was dispersing the fog when Agnes shouted.

'Reveal!'

The villagers watched in surprise as Marie's body twitched and shook. Ned, who was now awake, stared in horror at the scene before him. A hump swelled on her back, and her tiny waist ballooned into a round, saggy, fat stomach. Marie's feet burst out of her elegant pink slippers, and long hairy toes and crabby feet replaced her dainty white ones. Her arms grew fatter, and thick, black hairs sprouted along her arms and hands and down her fingers. Marie's fingers became claw-like, with long, hard yellow nails.

But that was nothing compared to her face. What had once been the most beautiful face anyone in Springfield had ever seen became the most grotesque. Marie's brilliant blue eyes turned red, and they bulged in their sockets. Her eyebrows were black and bushy and went without a break straight across her forehead. Her once-rosy lips were purple and cracked. Her high cheekbones, if they were still there, were not visible through her podgy fat cheeks.

As with her arms, thick, black hairs sprouted here and there along her chin and upper lip. Her beautiful blond hair fell out, leaving a shiny bald head. Marie drew back her purple lips and snarled, showing a mouth missing more teeth than it contained. In fact, the teeth that remained were so black that it was hard to spot them in her dark, cavernous mouth. As for warts, you couldn't have counted how many she had for it was hard to see a part of her face not covered with them.

If Agnes had thought this would make the villagers see that Marie was evil, she was badly mistaken. She threw her hands up in disbelief as the oohs and aahs from the crowd reached her ears. She even heard someone say, 'Now that's what I call a witch.' Naturally, they were terrified of her; Jimmy O'Loane even wet himself when he saw her. But to have such a witch in their village was the answer to all of their dreams. They would be the envy of not just the county but the whole country.

To say that Agnes was annoyed when she saw the looks of wonder and fear in the villager's faces would be an understatement. It was typical; even as a monster, this witch was still getting more respect than her. If she could rescue Ned and leave them to Marie, she would. But that was not her way; the only thing she could do was show them what had happened to the missing people.

Marie was lifting a fat, hairy hand to cast another curse when Agnes raised both her hands and sent a pillar of thick red smoke racing at her. The red smoke hit Marie and pinned her to the wall. Carefully, Agnes walked toward her. Marie screamed as Agnes lifted Marie's right hand and pulled off the bloodstone ring. As quick as lightning, Agnes pulled a rock from her pocket and smashed the ring to pieces.

'No!' she screamed as Marie started to cackle.

The villagers had no idea what was going on or why Agnes was sobbing into her hands. Taking advantage of the situation, Marie shot a bolt of lightning at Agnes, knocking her to the floor. In the matter of seconds, Marie had freed herself from the red mist and blasted a hole in the wall of the cottage.

Marie might have been quick, but Agnes wasn't going to be beaten. Before Marie could escape, Agnes opened her hands. Ropes catapulted across the room and tangled themselves around Marie. With a flick of her hand, Agnes brought the other witch to the ground. Agnes pulled her hands back, shortening the ropes, and dragged Marie back across the room. Agnes didn't expect another spell, but Marie's magic was powerful. Another bolt of lightning came blasting through the ropes, and if not for Ned's scream of warning Agnes would have been frazzled. Agnes swished her skirts out of the way and raised her hands. The bolt of lightning had scorched the ropes, and Marie was struggling to get free.

Agnes was furious. She was exhausted, and she had definitely had her fill of dodging spells. She threw herself down onto Marie. Then, in a very unladylike and extremely unwitchy way, Agnes punched, kneed, and elbowed Marie into submission.

'Where is it?' she screamed.

The villagers were confused; it was obvious that Agnes was looking for something, for she was searching through the filthy clothes of what they still considered their witch. Marie screamed and writhed as Agnes ripped a chain from around Marie's neck. Hanging from the chain was an ugly gold and amber pendant. Agnes grabbed a nearby piece of rubble and smashed the pendant. This time, she was sure she had it right.

# Chapter Sixteen
# Villagers Reunited

As the pendant broke, a circle of light burst from it, knocking the villagers onto their backs. The walls of the cottage crumbled, and the ceiling cracked, dropping Ned's cage heavily onto the floor. The thatched roof blew off in chunks, scattering thatch all over the garden. Even the plants and apple trees were flattened into greenish brown mulch. The once cute animals and birds were transformed into large, fat rats, bats, and savage-looking crows. Even the very ground shook. In fact, the energy it released was so great that the villagers in Crawfordshill felt it.

As the mob at Marie's window struggled to their feet, a series of cracks behind them compelled them to turn around. The statues in the garden were breaking apart. The villagers could hardly believe their eyes as they watched shadows growing from the splinters of crockery. The shadows began to take shape. Some became children, others formed the shape of adults, and some became animals and birds. More surprisingly, some even became fairies, but they disappeared into the woods as soon as they were free.

In the mass of beings, the villagers recognised those who had gone missing. They were amazed to see many strangers among those they knew. Not all the strangers were gypsies. Some of them looked like travelling salesmen, and some looked like businessmen from the city; some of them were even wearing old-fashioned clothes and wigs. More people had been abducted than anyone, other than Agnes, had guessed.

Those who had just been released looked dazed as they stared blankly around. Some of the children, spotting their parents, burst into tears. The gypsies, realising where they were, left as quickly as they could. But the strangers, totally bewildered, huddled together in a corner of the garden, looking around suspiciously.

The missing children and adults were almost crushed by the hugs of family and friends. The gabble of everyone talking together, telling of their adventures, filled the air for quite some time. Billy, the village dog, was released from his ceramic prison at the same time as everyone else. But unlike the villagers, he had more sense than to remain at the cottage which belonged to his gaoler. Anyway, it was a long time since he had been fed, and to Billy his stomach was the most important part of him.

Back in Agnes's cottage, Mr. Bradley found himself sitting on her kitchen table. He took a deep breath of free air before holding his nose and running for home. It was wonderful to be free, and thankfully the memory of the smell of Agnes's two-day-old cold sprout and spinach stew faded as he waddled home.

In next to no time, he was seated at his table with a good meal in front of him. It wasn't long before he was joined by Billy, begging for food. Some minutes later they were both chomping on a meal of sausages and potatoes. After being at Agnes's cottage for over a day, Mr. Bradley couldn't bring himself to cook any vegetable other than a few potatoes. In fact from that day, the only vegetable Mr. Bradley would eat was potatoes. The smell of any other vegetable cooking turned his complexion a strange shade of green.

Much to the disappointment of the villagers, after the pendant was smashed Marie didn't seem to have any powers left. But she became even more frantic to get away. She spat, bit, and kicked, leaving Agnes no alternative but to tie her to a chair. Even when there was no way for her to break free, she still struggled and screamed. Agnes, worried she might hurt herself, blew a sprinkle of dust into Marie's face. For a while, it seemed to calm her.

Agnes used the respite to free Ned from his prison in the birdcage.

'Wow, Agnes, that was amazing!' Ned squealed in delight. 'I thought you said you couldn't cast curses.'

Ned was jumping about her in delight.

'No, Ned,' Agnes corrected him. 'I said that I didn't cast curses, not that I couldn't. There's a big difference. Now stay still until I make sure you aren't hurt.'

He had a gash on his forehead and was very pale, but apart from that and some bruises he claimed he was fine. However, despite his reassurances, Agnes made sure he was really alright before she turned her attention back to Marie.

'I know what you are, Grobbler,' said Agnes. 'I also know you don't have any magic of your own.

You know you'll never beat me now that the pendant is gone, so if you stop trying to get away I'll loosen the ropes.'

Mr. and Mrs. Kenny, followed closely by Mr. O'Gill, had pushed their way through the mob of happy village folk and were standing in what was left of Marie's kitchen. Agnes smiled as Ned's parents almost crushed him death with their hugs, but she reserved a very cold look for Mr. O'Gill.

Mr. O'Gill very carefully laid down the pitchfork he was carrying. 'Madam, I just want to say I'm sorry. I made a grave mistake about you.'

'That's fine, Mr. O'Gill. I quite understand,' said Agnes politely.

Mr. O'Gill glanced between Agnes and Marie. 'Now, we'll take care of Marie. The villagers will be looking for justice.'

'No. I know what you mean by justice, and I can't allow that. I will take care of it,' said Agnes firmly.

'What are you going to do with her? She can't be allowed to go free!' argued Mr. O'Gill. He was not going to be bossed about by anyone, witch or not.

Agnes marched up to Mr. O'Gill and looked him squarely in the eye. It took all of Mr. O'Gill's nerve not to step back.

'That is no woman. It's not even human. It's a goblin called Grobbler. He's an evil and twisted goblin, I admit, but he's part of the fairy world all the same. I don't think you want to try and hang one of the fair folk. Can you imagine what you would be bringing on us all?'

'Still, Agnes, as the head of this village, I can't allow it to walk out of here.'

'Mr. O'Gill, you sound as if I am giving you a choice in this. Be very clear about this: I will do what needs to be done, and you will not get in my way. I'm sure you have seen what I am capable of. I really advise you not to cross me.' Agnes smiled sweetly, which made her statement even more frightening.

Ned was impressed; he had never heard Agnes speak with such authority. Secretly, Mr. O'Gill was also impressed, but he wasn't going to show it.

He tried to swallow the lump in his throat. 'Right. I will stand aside and let you do you what you need to . . . this time,' he added quietly.

Agnes glared at him, and he started to sweat. 'When I come back, there are going to be changes in this village,' she said.

'Yes, Agnes,' Mr. O'Gill answered meekly.

'I expect to be allowed to live quietly in my cottage. I also demand that you regard me as your witch. I think today I have earned the position.' Agnes, when she chose, could be quite formidable.

The villagers, having completed their reconciliations, were engrossed in what was happening between Mr. O'Gill and Agnes. Mr. O'Gill was aware of the faces gawping in through the windows. There was no way he was going to cross Agnes now. Judging by the eager expressions on his neighbours' faces, they were waiting for him to annoy her. There was no way he was going to be covered in boils or turned into a toad just for their amusement.

'That won't be a problem, Agnes. I think I speak for all the villagers when I say that it would be an honour to call you our witch,' Mr. O'Gill responded. Taking off his hat, he bowed to Agnes.

Then Agnes went back to the goblin and started to loosen the ropes so it could walk. It was crying loudly.

'Please don't take me back to the fairies,' Grobbler begged. 'You have no idea what they'll do to me.'

Agnes hesitated; she did pity Grobbler. At least, she did until it sunk its teeth into her arm and kicked her in the shin. She gave Grobbler a sharp slap around the ear and grabbed the ends of the ropes which still bound it. Agnes led the goblin from the cottage with difficulty as it continued to struggle. She aimed a small lightning bolt at its backside, causing it to jump a foot in the air. She couldn't help smiling as the villagers let up a cheer. As she passed Miss Robinson, she felt a tug on her sleeve. Agnes stopped, and Miss Robinson whispered quietly in her ear.

'If you don't mind, Witch Agnes, when you come back, could I try that cream you told me about?'

'Of course you may, Miss Robinson. Come and see me when I get back.'

'Agnes, you have to take me with you!' shouted Ned as he ran down the path after her.

Agnes saw the look of concern in his parents' faces. 'No, Ned, I'm sorry, but I can't take you with me. I don't know how long I will be gone or how I will be welcomed. The fair folk can be touchy. It's best if I go alone. Besides, someone has to look after my cottage and tend to my garden while I'm gone. Who else would I trust with that? Don't neglect your studies, now. All the books are yours until I get back.'

She kissed Ned on the top of the head and patted his cheek before leading the goblin off into the forest to meet up with the escaped fairies she knew were waiting for her. The villagers watched her until she disappeared through the trees before starting for their homes. Ned continued watching long after everyone else. The intermittent flashes of lightning bolts gave away her position in the forest for quite a while. Ned's mum put her arm around his shoulders and gently led him away from Marie's cottage.

'Don't worry, Ned. She'll be back soon,' said his dad.

'Sure she will!' agreed his uncle.

Ned wondered if they were right. He was happy that the missing people had been found, but he was sad that his only friend had gone. Before he had met Agnes, being alone had never really bothered him, but now everything had changed. Even the gift of a library of books didn't console him.

# Chapter Seventeen
## Agnes Returns

Now that the goblin was gone, the children were once again allowed to leave their homes. They spent all day playing games and enjoying their freedom. The school had remained closed, for once Miss Meek had ceased being a statue, she had packed her bags and left Springfield. As Miss Meek and some of the strangers left the village, others who had been scared away returned.

Not all of the strangers had left the village; many of them had received invitations from the villagers to stay. After Agnes's departure, the villagers discovered that Grobbler had been abducting people for years. In fact, some of the people had been imprisoned for hundreds of years. Although the people of Springfield had behaved badly towards Agnes, they really weren't bad people. They were truly sorry for everyone Grobbler had cursed; they even felt somewhat responsible as they had opened their doors so readily to Marie.

The villagers also realised that if it hadn't been for Agnes, their loved ones might have remained garden ornaments until the end of time. So to show their appreciation for all Agnes had done, a team of men went to her cottage and repaired the door they had smashed. They even put up shelves for her library of books. It was important for them to show Agnes how sorry they were about the way they had behaved in the past. Ned found that he didn't need to do very much around the cottage. The men weeded the garden, whitewashed the walls of the cottage, and rethatched the roof. A troop of women went daily to clean the cottage. Someone had even taken the trouble to light the fire every day to keep the damp away.

Still, every day Ned visited Agnes's cottage. Each day he came away disappointed that she had not returned. Then on the sixth day of her absence, as he approached her cottage, he was welcomed by the scent of boiling cabbage. Ned ran straight into her kitchen and threw his arms around her as she stood at her stove. Agnes laughed as she returned his embrace.

Over a refreshing cup of mint tea, Ned quizzed Agnes about the last few days.

'You know, Ned, I never thought that I would ever admit this, but if I had paid more attention to my mother, I could have stopped this a long time ago. For a long time I had this niggling feeling that something about these disappearances was vaguely familiar. That night in the smithy, I had a dream about a story my mum had once told me. Of course, I thought her stories were pointless fairy tales, so I didn't really listen. I'm actually surprised that I picked up as much as I did.'

'I don't understand. Is Grobbler in a fairy tale?' Ned asked.

'Not the kind of fairy tales you are thinking of. According to my mum, the stories she told me were actual fairy histories. The one about Grobbler began hundreds of years ago. It's said that after years of his wickedness, the fairies stripped him of his power and held him captive in the fairy world. It seems that for a long time he fought against his imprisonment, but over the years he seemed to mellow. He showed such remorse for all he had done that Kieran, who is the king of the fairies, granted him certain privileges. Time and again he won favours with the fairies until Kieran made him his personal servant. It was a position which gave him a lot of freedom in the fairy world.

'He lived that way for such long time that the fairies started to forget why he had been punished in the first place. Of course, my mum said that's what he was waiting for. Once he had their trust, he stole a very powerful artefact. That's when I stopped listening. I remembered that is was a piece of jewellery but had no idea what it looked like. All I knew was that it was the source of his magic and without it he was powerless. The ring was an obvious choice for me because it was so ugly and seemed so out of place. You have no idea how scared I was when I smashed it and nothing happened.'

'I thought you were brilliant,' said Ned honestly. 'I have to admit, I had no idea that you were so powerful.'

'Well, neither had I. But I guess sparring with my mum all those years made fighting Grobbler child's play.'

'You fought with your mum?' choked Ned.

'Yes, of course I did. She was crazy . . . still is. There wasn't a day when she didn't hurl half a dozen spells at me. I had to protect myself. She said I would thank her one day. I guess she was right, as usual, but I'm not telling her that. She loves saying "I told you" so far too much.'

'Where's Grobbler now?'

'He's locked up in a fairy dungeon. I reckon he'll be there for a really long time. That pendant he stole was kept in an enchanted cave, and they're still unsure how he broke in; he would have needed to use magic to get across the seal. When I left, they were still quizzing him about it, but he's so stubborn there's no way he will ever tell them.'

'Why didn't they go after him when he escaped?'

'They did, but they never found him. The power of the pendant helped to hide him. Whenever they closed in on him, he disappeared, along with one or two of the fairies. We know now what happened to them.'

'How did you defeat him?' Ned asked. 'Are you stronger than they are?'

'No, I'm not. I think that's why I got the better of him. He underestimated me. If the fairies had have been closing in on him, he would have done a disappearing act. But he didn't think I was that much of a threat.'

'Where is the entrance to the fairy domain?'

'Never you mind. That kind of information can be dangerous. The fairies keep that a great secret, and they don't like non-magic folk nosing about without an invite.'

'But how did you know?' Ned asked.

'All witches know,' stated Agnes.

'Did the fairies welcome you? I'll bet they were impressed you had captured Grobbler when he had evaded them all this time.'

'Well, they were very gracious, and that's all I have to say on that subject,' said Agnes.

It was obvious to Ned that Agnes didn't want to talk about her time in the fairy world. What he didn't know was that one week here was equivalent to one month in the fairy world. Agnes had been there for six months and was glad to be home. She had found it difficult to leave. The fairies were very hospitable, and because they owed her a great deal, they didn't want her to leave. It had taken all her powers of persuasion to convince them to let her go.

'I really missed you. The days seemed to just drag in.'

'I missed you too. Now put on your coat,' Agnes said, and she lifted a bottle from a shelf.

'What's in the bottle?' asked Ned.

'Ear drops. I want to make sure your uncle can hear perfectly when I tell him I am going to take over as teacher of your school.'

Agnes took Ned's hand and walked with him to the village. And as Ned remarked to Agnes, it's sometimes nice to get everything you dream of.

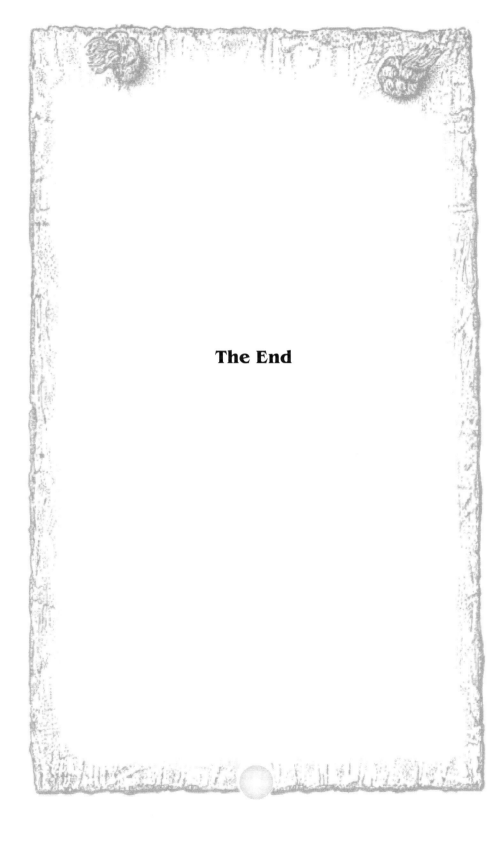

**The End**